AF294974

Doctors
at the
Funfair
Ulrich Germania

Imprint

Book title:
Doctors at the Funfair

Subtitle:
Not a typical doctor's story, but somehow

Series:
Romantic Encounters at the Funfair

AI Note:
AI generated story, initiated and revised by the author
Translated from German into American English by an AI.

Author:
Ulrich Germania © 2025

Publisher:
BoD · Books on Demand GmbH, In de Tarpen 42,
22848 Norderstedt, bod@bod.de

Print:
Libri Plureos GmbH,
Friedensallee 273, 22763 Hamburg

ISBN: 978-3-7597-6922-0

Table of contents

The Funfair 7

Nurse Mary 9

Dr. Marty 10

Encounter at the pony carousel............................ 11

Emma and Mary 16

Accident with a bang 20

Near the dance floor 23

Doctor Bernie 26

Back to live music 30

Emma with Bernie 32

Mary and Marty 34

End of the fair 37

In the Latino bar.. 39

More Books by the Author 46

Picture credits:

The images on the book cover and the illustrations in the book were generated by AI and modified using programs for photo manipulation.

AI Note:

Author Ulrich Germania came up with the characters and the plot, the AI wrote the story, then it was revised and improved. The translation from German into American English was also done by an AI.
The translation was checked and approved.

The Funfair

It was a balmy summer evening on the day when a funfair opened in the town once again, after a long time. For two weeks, the fair would enrich the city with colorful lights, a sea of colors and sounds. The smell of candy floss and roasted almonds filled the air, while the cheerful laughter of visitors filled the atmosphere. There were rides spinning and swinging everywhere, from the wild roller coaster to the cozy Ferris wheel, which offered a magnificent view over the entire fair and large parts of the city.

The kitsch stalls were packed with all kinds of knick-knacks and souvenirs, from glittering snow globes to handmade jewelry.

Children ran excitedly from stand to stand, their eyes shining with joy and curiosity.

The food stalls offered a variety of delicacies, from hearty sausages to sweet crêpes, which were freshly prepared in front of the hungry visitors.

Adults sat in the beer gardens, enjoyed a cool drink and listened to live music from a small stage.

The funfair was a place where people met, laughed and forgot the worries of everyday life for the duration of their visit.

Here, in the midst of this colorful hustle and bustle, a love story was to begin that would outlast the fairground days.

Nurse Mary

Mary, a 23-year-old nurse, was on her way into town to meet her work colleague and best friend Emma in a chic café. She was sitting on the streetcar, watching the passing scenery, when the streetcar suddenly stopped right in front of the fairground. She spontaneously decided to get out and take a quick look around.

The sight of the colorful lights and the cheerful atmosphere immediately captivated her. She could smell the scent of candy floss and roasted almonds and hear the laughter of the people around her.

She enthusiastically called her friend Emma and suggested that they meet at the funfair instead. Emma immediately agreed and set off.

In the meantime, Mary strolled around the fairground, letting herself be carried away by the impressions and enjoying the carefree atmosphere.

Dr. Marty

Marty, a 28-year-old doctor, was working at the accident assistance stand at the fairground. He was tall and athletic, with short, dark brown hair and a friendly smile that inspired confidence. Marty had volunteered to work at the funfair because he loved helping people and because he didn't want to do emergency doctor duty in a sterile hospital, but in the cheerful atmosphere at the funfair.

His stand was clearly visible, with a large red cross and a white tent where he and his small team provided first aid. Marty was always attentive and ready to intervene immediately in the event of minor injuries or accidents. He had a calm and reassuring manner that made people feel they were in good hands.

Although he had a lot to do, he always took a moment to observe the happy faces of the funfair visitors and soak up the positive energy.

Little did he know that this evening would bring him more than just a few hours of work.

Encounter at the pony carousel

While Mary waited for her friend Emma, she strolled leisurely around the fairground. Suddenly she heard the typical neighing of horses. Curious, she followed the sound and discovered a small area where children could ride ponies. The ponies trotted leisurely in a circle while the children sat on their backs, laughing and waving cheeringly to their parents.

Just as Mary approached to watch what was happening, it happened. A small child sitting on one of the ponies suddenly lost its balance. Mary saw the child tip forward and finally slip off the pony. A startled cry went through the crowd as the child fell to the ground.

Mary felt her heart beat faster. Without hesitation, she ran to the scene of the accident while the child's parents also rushed over.

"I'm a nurse," Mary explained to the parents as she knelt next to the crying child and wanted to check whether it had hurt itself when it fell off the pony.

The child was lying on the floor crying and calling for its mother. The mother picked the child up and let it sit in her arms while Mary said to her mother: "We should check that the child didn't break anything when it fell."

The mother nodded.

At that moment, someone else also rushed to help. It was Marty, the doctor from the accident service responsible for the funfair.

"Hello, I'm the doctor from the casualty department," he introduced himself and everyone recognized him immediately: he was wearing white jeans, a white shirt and a white jacket with a red cross embroidered on it.

Marty looked at Mary, who was standing worriedly by the mother and child.

"Everything's fine, I'll take care of it," he said with a reassuring smile.

Mary nodded and took a step back to give him space but stayed close by in case she was needed.

With a calm voice and professional composure, Marty took charge of the situation.

He nodded to Mary, then said to the child's mother:

"The lady is right, we should check the child for injuries."

The mother calmed the crying child and Marty began to examine it carefully for injuries.

Mary watched in fascination as Marty acted with a mixture of competence and compassion. She knew that she had just witnessed a special moment.

While Marty examined the child, he spoke softly and reassuringly to the child.

"It looks like you've just picked up a few scrapes. Nothing serious, but we'll make sure your little ache heals quickly."

The child stopped crying and looked at Marty with wide eyes as he carefully tended to the small abrasions.

Mary could see how skillful and sensitive Marty was, and she was attracted to his calm manner.

When Marty had finished, the mother put the child back on his own feet and the parents thanked Marty with a handshake.

"Take good care of yourselves," Marty said with a smile before turning to Mary.

"I'm glad you were there so quickly," he said. "By the way, I'm Marty, the official accident doctor at the funfair, but otherwise I work at the university hospital."

"Mary," she replied and smiled back. "I'm a nurse at the Theresien Klinik, I didn't know there was a doctor at the fair. So I wanted to make sure there was nothing wrong with the child."

"Ahh, you're a nurse? That explains why you stayed so calm," Marty said appreciatively and added:

"It's always good to have someone with a medical background nearby to provide first aid until a doctor arrives."

Mary felt her cheeks flush slightly. "It was impressive to watch you. You did a really good job."

Marty laughed softly.

"Thank you. It's nice to hear that. Maybe we'll see you again later at the funfair?"

Mary nodded. "I'd like that."

With a smile, they parted ways, but both hoped that they would meet again.

Emma and Mary

Mary was strolling through the fairground again when her cell phone suddenly rang. The name 'Emma' was on the display.

"Hello Mary, I'm at the funfair now too. Where are you? Where can we meet?"

"The best place is the Ferris wheel, there's only one of them and you can't miss it," suggested Mary and the two girls made their way to the Ferris wheel.

Before she had even reached the Ferris wheel, Mary spotted her friend Emma in the crowd. Emma waved cheerfully to her and made her way through the crowds until she finally reached Mary.

"Hey, Mary! What a crazy idea for us to meet at the funfair," Emma exclaimed and gave her friend a big hug.

Mary was beaming all over her face.

"Emma, you won't believe what just happened! I met someone and it was so exciting!"

She could hardly contain her excitement and immediately began to tell the story.

"Well, I was on my way to the ponies when I saw a little child fall off a horse. It was so terrible! I immediately ran to give first aid, but then someone else arrived - a doctor called Marty. He took such good care of the child, it was really impressive."

Emma listened attentively and nodded enthusiastically. "Wow, that sounds like something out of a movie! And what was this Marty like?"

Mary smiled dreamily.

"He was tall, good looking and had that friendly smile that instantly instills confidence. He was so calm and professional as he cared for the child. I watched him with fascination."

Emma giggled. "That sounds like you've already fallen in love. And then what happened?"

"After he had looked after the child, he thanked me for the first aid and we had a quick chat. He asked me if I would see him again later at the funfair. I said yes, of course," said Mary with a broad grin.

Emma clapped her hands.

"That's fantastic! Maybe this is the beginning of a relationship. I'm so excited to see what happens next!"

Mary nodded. "Me too. But now let's enjoy the fair and see what else the evening brings."

The two friends set off to explore the various attractions at the funfair, while Mary kept thinking about her encounter with Marty.

Emma also remembered the story Mary had told her and was curious. She really wanted to know what Marty looked like.

"Mary, I'm curious to see what your Marty looks like. Let's just go to the accident assistance stand so I can see him," she suggested.

Mary hesitated briefly, but then she nodded. "Good idea, Emma. Let's go there. Maybe he's still there."

The two friends made their way through the colorful hustle and bustle of the fair. They walked past the rides and food stalls until they finally reached the accident assistance stand. They couldn't miss the big red cross and the white tent.

As they approached, they saw Marty applying a plaster to a young boy's knee. His calm and professional manner was immediately recognizable.

"There he is," Mary whispered excitedly. "That's Marty."

Emma looked at him attentively and nodded approvingly. "He is very handsome, Mary. And he seems to be doing a good job, too."

Mary smiled proudly. "Yes, he does. I'm so glad I met him."

The two girls watched Marty for a while before plunging back into the hustle and bustle of the funfair.

Mary couldn't shake off the feeling that this evening was something very special and that her story with Marty had only just begun.

Accident with a bang

Mary and Emma continued to stroll through the funfair when suddenly a loud bang filled the air. They both turned around, startled, and saw a small children's carousel which had come to an abrupt halt.

A child sitting on the back of a plastic elephant had fallen off the elephant due to the carousel's emergency braking. It was now screaming in pain, or because it was frightened.

Mary reacted instinctively and ran to the scene of the accident. She knelt down next to the crying child and began to calm it down.

"It's going to be okay, I'm here to help you," she said gently, checking the child for injuries. Fortunately, it only seemed to have a few scrapes and bruises.

At that moment, Marty appeared, who had also heard the bang and the child's cry and immediately set off.

Marty saw Mary, who was already with the child, and smiled approvingly.

"You're faster than me again," he said jokingly as he knelt down next to her.

"I couldn't help it," Mary replied, smiling back. "It looks like the child will only get a few bruises, but I wanted to make sure everything was okay."

Marty nodded and began to examine the child as well.

"You've done a good job, Mary. Nothing seems to have happened, apart from a few bruises I don't notice anything. But we'll check again to make sure it hasn't sprained its ankles or wrists." Together they looked after the child and reassured the worried parents.

After examining the child and finding no injuries, Mary and Marty stood up and looked at each other.

"You're really impressive, Mary," said Marty. "It's nice to see you taking care of others."

Mary blushed slightly.

"Thank you, Marty. It's also nice to have someone like you here. You're a great doctor."

Marty smiled. "Maybe we should meet up again later and have a chat. I'd like to find out more about you."

Mary nodded. "I'd be happy to. When do you get off work?"

Marty looked at his watch and replied:

"I'm off work in an hour. How about we meet at the big stage then? There's a live band playing there and we could have a chat."

Mary smiled. "That sounds like a plan. I'm looking forward to it."

"See you later," said Marty and said goodbye with a wave of his hand.

Near the dance floor

Mary and Emma strolled to the big stage, where the live band had just returned to the stage after a break and were tuning their instruments again before the first notes rang out. As soon as the first song was played, people were dancing to the rhythm of the music.

The two friends were enjoying the cheerful atmosphere when suddenly a drunk man approached them. He staggered and slurred unintelligible words as he tried to molest Mary and Emma.

Mary felt her heart beating faster. She tried to ignore the drunk and turn away from him, but he wouldn't let up. Emma stood protectively in front of her friend, but the drunk became more and more insistent.

The situation threatened to escalate when Marty suddenly appeared.

Marty had just finished work and was on his way to the stage to meet Mary.

When he saw the scene, he didn't hesitate for a second. With a determined look, he stood in front of Mary and Emma to protect the girls. "Leave them alone," he ordered the man in a firm voice.

The drunk stared at Marty, his eyes narrowed with rage. Without warning, he lashed out and punched Marty in the face with his fist. The blow was violent and Marty staggered back a step as the drunk quickly disappeared into the crowd.

Mary gave a startled cry and immediately rushed to Marty.

"Marty, are you all right?" she asked anxiously as she examined his face. There was a small laceration on his cheek and it looked as if it was about to bleed, but Marty smiled bravely.

Mary took a paper handkerchief and pressed it on the wound until she was sure that she had prevented any bleeding.

"It's all right, Mary," said Marty reassuringly. "What's more important is that you're both safe."

Mary felt a mixture of relief and admiration for Marty.

"Thank you for helping us," she said quietly. "You're really brave."

Marty smiled and put a hand on her shoulder.

"I would do the same thing over and over again, Mary. Now let's have a nice evening and enjoy the music."

Together they walked back to the stage, where the band was now in full swing.

Doctor Bernie

Unfortunately, the small laceration on Marty's cheek started to bleed and Mary immediately became concerned.

"Marty, your wound is bleeding again. Let's go to the accident assistance stand so that you can be treated," she said firmly.

Marty nodded and smiled bravely. "Good idea, Mary. I don't want it to get any worse."

Mary handed Marty a paper handkerchief, which Marty pressed to his cheek. Together, Mary, Marty and Emma made their way to the accident assistance stand. When they arrived, they saw that Marty's colleague Bernie was now working there.

Bernie was an experienced paramedic who immediately recognized that something was wrong because Marty was pressing a handkerchief to his face.

"Marty, what happened?" asked Bernie worriedly when he saw the bleeding wound on Marty's cheek.

"I had a little altercation with a drunk," Marty explained, shrugging his shoulders. "It's nothing serious, but he hit me with his fist."

Marty pointed to Mary and said: "That's Mary, a nurse, she stopped the first bleeding, but now the wound is bleeding again."

Bernie nodded and led Marty to a chair. "Sit down, I'll take care of this."

He immediately began to clean and treat the wound while Mary and Emma looked on anxiously.

Because Bernie wanted to hear more about the little argument, Emma told him in detail how the drunk had harassed her until Marty intervened.

"Marty was very brave," Emma said appreciatively at the end of her story.

Marty smiled faintly. "It was the right thing to do. I wanted the drunk to stop bothering you, and I succeeded."

Bernie worked with routine and concentration. With practiced hand movements and a drug that could stop bleeding, he stopped the bleeding

"That should be better now and shouldn't start bleeding again," he said reassuringly to Marty as he stuck a small plaster on his cheek.

"Take good care of yourself and avoid any more punches to the face," he added with a wink.

Mary watched the care carefully and was relieved.

"Thank you, Bernie. I'm so glad you're here and were able to help."

Bernie smiled. "No problem at all. It's always good to have friends who look out for you."

Suddenly, Mary stepped closer to Marty and smiled at him.

"It'll heal even faster in a minute," she said and gave him a gentle peck on the cheek, right next to the plaster.

Marty smiled gratefully and felt his heart beat faster.

"Thank you, Mary. That was the best medicine," he said quietly.

Emma, who had been watching the scene, grinned broadly. "You two are really cute together," she remarked and winked at Mary.

Mary blushed slightly, but she couldn't hide her smile.

"Let's go back to the stage and enjoy the music," she suggested. "I think we still have a nice evening ahead of us."

Together, the three of them made their way back to the big stage, where the live band was in full swing. The cheerful music and exuberant atmosphere quickly made them forget the previous incidents.

Despite, or perhaps because of the incident, Mary and Marty felt that their bond had become stronger. They knew that they could rely on each other if anything happened.

Back to live music

Mary and Marty danced to the rock music played by the live band. The cheerful music and exuberant atmosphere made them forget everything around them. They laughed, spun to the beat of the music and enjoyed being close to each other. With every song that was played, they felt their connection grow stronger and they fell more and more in love with each other.

Emma stood a little apart and watched her friend and Marty. She was happy for Mary, but couldn't help feeling like a third wheel. As she looked at the two of them, she kept thinking about Bernie. His friendly and professional manner had left a lasting impression on her.

Emma sighed softly and decided to enjoy the evening anyway, and perhaps there would still be an opportunity for her to get to know Bernie better.

With a determined smile, she set off to get herself a drink, then she came up with the idea of buying two drinks, one for herself and one for Bernie.

Mary and Marty noticed Emma's absence and took a quick look around. "Where's Emma gone?" asked Marty worriedly.

"I think she wanted to get a drink," Mary replied. "I hope she doesn't feel left out."

Marty smiled reassuringly. "Don't worry, Mary. Emma is a strong woman. And who knows, maybe she'll meet someone special tonight."

Mary nodded and smiled. "You're right. Let's enjoy the moment."

They continued to dance together as the music captivated them and they enjoyed the evening to the full.

Emma with Bernie

Emma got herself two soft drinks, a Coke and a lemonade, and went to the accident assistance stand. She wanted to keep Bernie company while he was on call as an emergency doctor. When she arrived, she saw Bernie, who was taking a short break and sat down on a chair.

"Hello Bernie," Emma called out cheerfully and waved to him. "I thought I'd come over and keep you company for a while."

Bernie smiled when he saw her. "Hello Emma, that's a nice surprise."

Emma said: "Look, I've just bought a Coke and a lemonade. What do you want to drink? Take your pick."

"Wow, thank you. I'll have the Coke. Why don't you sit with me?"

Emma took a seat, handed Bernie the Coke and said: "I hope you're not too busy tonight."

Bernie shook his head. "Fortunately, it was pretty quiet, apart from a few minor injuries. It's nice of you to come and see me. It's always good to have someone to talk to."

The two of them talked about the funfair, their experiences and laughed at the funny stories they could tell. Emma felt comfortable in Bernie's company and realized that she was becoming more and more interested in him.

As they talked, Bernie noticed how attentive and empathetic Emma was. He enjoyed her company and was glad to have someone to talk to. Time flew by and they both realized that they were forming a special bond with each other.

Mary and Marty

Meanwhile, at the stage: 20 minutes before midnight, as the end of the funfair approached, the live band suddenly stopped the rock music. The singer stepped up to the microphone and spoke to the guests:

"For the last 20 minutes of our concert, we will now play romantic songs for lovers," he announced.

People giggled sheepishly and the atmosphere changed abruptly. The lights dimmed and the first soft sounds of a romantic song filled the air.

Mary and Marty looked at each other, a smile on their faces. Without saying a word, Marty took Mary's hand and gently pulled her closer to him.

They began to dance slowly, their movements in harmony with the music. The world around them seemed to disappear and it was just the two of them.

Mary laid her head on Marty's shoulder and felt her heart beat faster.

Marty held her tightly and enjoyed the moment of closeness and tenderness.

The romantic songs created a magical atmosphere and Mary and Marty felt as if they were the only people in the world. With every song that was played, they fell more and more in love with each other. It was an unforgettable moment.

As the last notes of the romantic music faded away, Mary and Marty were standing on the dance floor in a tight embrace. The world around them seemed to stand still and it was just the two of them. The soft sounds of the last song were still ringing in their ears as they looked deep into each other's eyes.

Mary felt her heart beat faster and she could feel Marty's warm breath on her skin. Her hands rested on his shoulders while his arms held her tightly. It was a moment full of magic and tenderness, and she knew that this moment was something very special.

Slowly, Marty leaned down towards her and Mary closed her eyes. Their lips met in a soft, tender kiss that expressed all the feelings they had for each other.

It was a kiss full of love and affection that made time stand still for a moment.

The people around them seemed to disappear and there was only Mary and Marty left, lost in this magical moment.

When they finally broke away from each other, they looked deep into each other's eyes and knew that this kiss was the beginning of a special love.

Mary and Marty were sitting closely together on the beer benches by the stage. The last visitors to the fair were slowly making their way home, but the two of them just couldn't stop hugging and kissing. The romantic music had created a magical atmosphere and they enjoyed every moment of their closeness.

The fairground lights began to fade and the sounds of the rides gradually died away. But for Mary and Marty, time seemed to stand still.

They spoke quietly to each other, laughed and exchanged tender glances. It was as if the world around them no longer existed.

End of the fair

In the meantime, Bernie had closed the accident assistance stand and made his way to the stage with Emma. Emma wanted to get back to her friend Mary and hoped that she was still there.

When they arrived at the stage, they saw Mary and Marty sitting closely together on the beer benches.

Bernie smiled and turned to Emma.

"It looks like the two of them had a really nice evening," he said quietly.

Emma nodded and smiled too. "Yes, they did. It's nice to see how happy they are."

Bernie and Emma sat down on a nearby bench and watched the two of them. They enjoyed the quiet atmosphere and each other's company. Bernie sensed that a special connection had also developed between him and Emma, and he was curious to see where it would lead.

Mary and Marty finally noticed the presence of Bernie and Emma and waved to them. "Come here, sit with us," Marty called out cheerfully.

Bernie and Emma got up and joined them. They spent the last few minutes of the fair together, laughing and swapping stories.

Finally, a man from security came and kindly asked the two couples to leave the fairground, as the fair was now closed.

Mary, Marty, Emma and Bernie nodded in understanding and made their way to the exit.

In the Latino bar

Marty offered to take everyone to the city center in his car.

"How about we end the evening in a Latino bar? I know a great place where a DJ plays salsa music until 5 a.m.," he suggested.

The others agreed enthusiastically and so they drove into the city center together. They laughed a lot during the journey and the atmosphere was exuberant.

When they entered the Latino bar, they were greeted by the rhythmic music and lively atmosphere.

The bar was full of people dancing to South American and Cuban salsa music. The cheerful, Caribbean atmosphere immediately captivated the four of them. They found a table near the dance floor and ordered drinks while enjoying the atmosphere.

Marty asked Mary if she could dance Salsa, and she said yes. The two were delighted that again they had found something they had in common.

Mary and Marty took to the dance floor. They danced to the hot rhythms of salsa music, their movements in perfect harmony. It was as if they had danced Salsa together many times before and they enjoyed every second of it.

Emma and Bernie watched the two of them and smiled. "They look so happy," Emma said.

Bernie nodded. "Yes, they do. And I'm glad we can spend this evening together."

Emma smiled and took Bernie's hand. "Let's dance too," she suggested.

Bernie hesitated briefly. "But I can't dance Salsa," he said, and Emma laughed: "Me neither, but I want to dance."

Bernie laughed and followed Emma onto the dance floor. They danced together in an improvised way to the rousing sounds of salsa music and felt their connection grow stronger and stronger.

The night flew by and the four of them enjoyed every moment in the Latino bar.

Towards the end of the evening, the DJ took the microphone and announced: "In 30 minutes it's closing time, from now on I'll be playing romantic rumba music for lovers."

The guests in the Latino bar laughed sheepishly, but they were delighted that the atmosphere of the Latino party was now becoming more intimate and romantic. The lights were dimmed, and the first soft sounds of rumba music filled the room.

Bernie and Emma were still on the dance floor. Although neither of them could dance the rumba, they decided to just stay in time with the music and enjoy the moment. They moved slowly and carefully, their eyes locked on each other.

The music created a magical atmosphere, and they could feel their hearts beating to the same rhythm.

As they danced, they got closer and closer. Bernie gently placed his hands on Emma's hips, and she put her arms around his neck. Their movements became more synchronized, and they felt as if they had always danced together.

The world around them seemed to disappear and it was just the two of them.

The romantic music and the closeness to each other made their feelings for each other grow stronger and stronger. Finally, as a particularly emotional song played, they looked deep into each other's eyes.

Without saying a word, Bernie slowly leaned down towards Emma and she closed her eyes. Their lips met in a soft, tender kiss that expressed all the pent-up feelings they had for each other today.

It was a kiss full of love and affection that made time stand still for a moment. The world around them disappeared and there was only Bernie and Emma, lost in this magical moment.

When they finally broke away from each other, they looked deep into each other's eyes and knew that this kiss was the beginning of a very special love.

By the end of the evening, there were only couples kissing on the dance floor. The romantic rumba music filled the room and the atmosphere was full of love and tenderness.

Bernie and Emma held each other tightly and enjoyed the last few minutes of the music, while Mary and Marty also danced closely together and kept giving each other tender kisses.

When the music stopped and the last notes faded away, the two couples were still sitting at the table enjoying their drinks. The atmosphere was relaxed and full of affection as they chatted quietly and reflected on the magical evening. The waiter finally came up to them and kindly asked them to leave as the restaurant was now closed.

The four of them quickly exchanged phone numbers to stay in touch. Mary took out her cell phone and set up a WhatsApp group called "Funfair".

"So, we can all keep in touch and see each other again," she said with a laugh as she invited the others into the group.

Suddenly Emma said: "Do you know why this was a very special evening? Because two nurses and two doctors didn't meet in hospital, but at the funfair!"

Everyone laughed, and Bernie remarked: "What luck, otherwise our story would be the stuff of a cheesy doctor's novel!"

Whereupon everyone laughed so loudly again that the waiter came back to the table again and remind them that they had to leave now.

Marty offered to drive everyone home. The others gratefully accepted the offer and made their way to the parking lot.

First Marty drove Emma home. She thanked him warmly and kissed Bernie goodbye. "It was a wonderful evening. I'm already looking forward to our next meeting," she said before getting out of the car.

Then Marty drove Bernie home. Bernie also thanked him and said goodbye with a firm handshake. "Thank you, Marty. It was a great evening. See you soon," he said before getting out of the car.

Eventually, Marty and Mary drove on together. The roads were quiet, and they enjoyed the silence and the closeness to each other.

"My place or your place?" asked Marty, not caring what Mary's answer would be.

More Books by the Author

If you enjoyed this romantic, kitschy fairground story, then you are sure to enjoy other short stories that Ulrich Germania has come up with.

Many stories by the author tell of romantic encounters in unusual places.

AI-Note: For the following stories applies: Ulrich Germania came up with the characters and the plot, the AI wrote the story, and then the author revised and improved it.

Fair of Hearts
Short, kitschy fairground story

Doctors at the funfair
Not a doctor's story, but somehow.
(this book)

The Goddess of Love at the Fair
A fair with a mystical flair

In Love with Costumes
Romantic encounters at a cosplay event

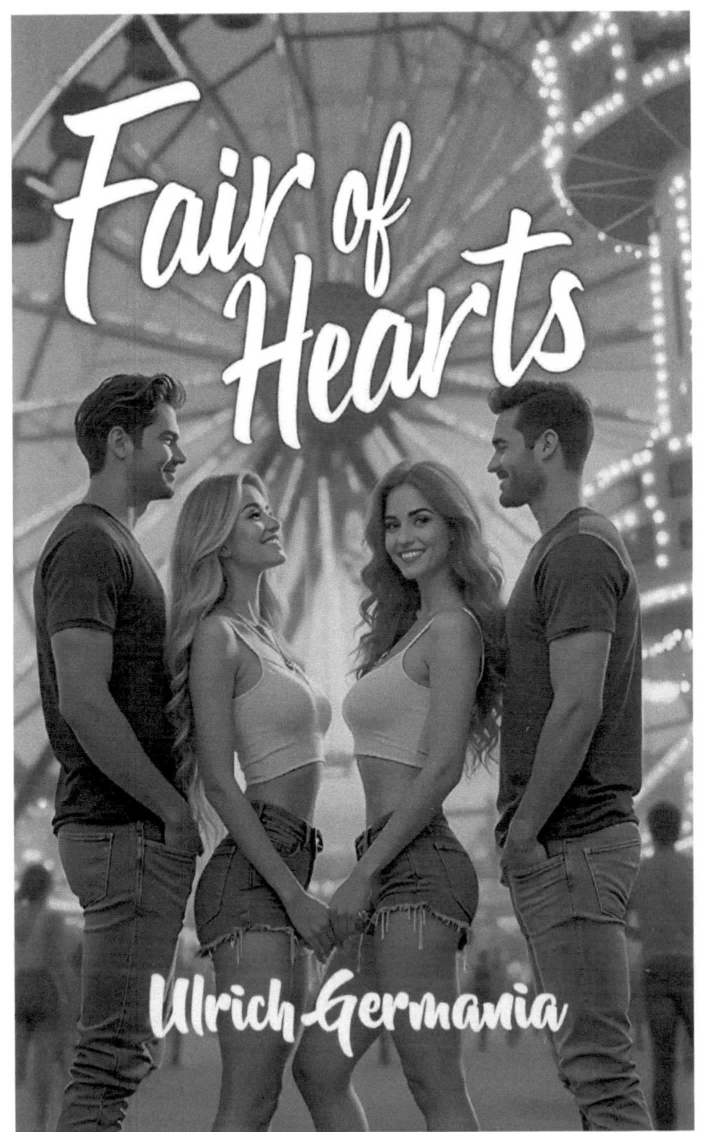

Fair of Hearts
Ulrich Germania

The Goddess of Love
at the Funfair
Ulrich Germania